A Basic Training, Caring & Understanding Library

Healthy Skin & Coat: Dogs

Approved by the A.S.P.C.A.

Dunbar Gram, DVM

Published in association with T.F.H. Publications, Inc.,
the world's largest and most respected publisher of pet literature

Chelsea House Publishers
Philadelphia

A Basic Training, Caring & Understanding Library

Publisher's Note: All of the photographs in this book have been coated with FOTOGLAZE™ finish, a special lamination that imparts a new dimension of colorful gloss to the photographs.

Reinforced Library Binding & Super-Highest Quality Boards

This edition © 1998 Chelsea House Publishers, a division of Main Line Book Company.

© yearBOOKS, Inc.

135798642
Library of Congress Cataloging-in-Publication Data applied for 0-7910-4818-7.

HEALTHY SKIN AND COAT FOR DOGS

by DUNBAR GRAM, DVM

yearBOOKS,INC.

Dr. Herbert R. Axelrod,
Founder & Chairman

Dominique De Vito
Chief Editor

Carolynne Van Houten
Editor

yearBOOKS are all photo composed, color separated and designed on Scitex equipment in Neptune, N.J. with the following staff:

DIGITAL PRE-PRESS
Patricia Northrup
Supervisor

Robert Onyrscuk
Jose Reyes

COMPUTER ART
Patti Escabi
Sandra Taylor Gale
Candida Moreira
Joanne Muzyka
Francine Shulman

ADVERTISING SALES
Nancy S. Rivadeneira
Advertising Sales Director
Cheryl J. Blyth
Advertising Account Manager
Amy Manning
Advertising Director
Sandy Cutillo
Advertising Coordinator

©yearBOOKS, Inc.
1 TFH Plaza
Neptune, N.J. 07753
Completely manufactured in
Neptune, N.J.
USA

Cover design by Sherise Buhagiar

CONTENTS

Photo Credits: Dr. Diane Bevier, Isabelle Francais, Dunbar Gram, DVM, Greer Laboratories, Dr. Tom Manning.

WHAT ARE QUARTERLIES?

Books, the usual way information of this sort is transmitted, can be too slow. Sometimes, by the time a book is written and published, the material contained therein is a year or two old...and no new material has been added during that time. Only a book in a magazine form can bring breaking stories and current information. A magazine is streamlined in production, so we have adopted certain magazine publishing techniques in the creation of this Dog Quarterly. Magazines can also be less expensive than books because they are supported by advertising. To combine these assets into a great publication, we are issuing this Quarterly in both magazine and book format at different prices.

Your dog will always look to you to ensure his health and welfare.

INTRODUCTION

This publication provides information regarding canine skin and various skin conditions. It is by no means complete or a substitute for veterinary care. The cause of a pet's skin problem is often difficult, if not impossible, to determine without performing diagnostic tests and/or monitoring response to treatment. In some patients more that one disease may be causing the problem.

Infections and other diseases may come and go either with therapy or other factors. Additionally, a normal test result at one time does not mean that the disease was not present at a different time. Reevaluations by a veterinarian may reveal different symptoms of the same diseases or the presence of a new disease. It is important to differentiate these two possibilities from the possibility of treatment failure.

With many chronic and incurable diseases, several different treatment options may be attempted before finding one that works for each individual. If symptoms are caused by an unusual, chronic, or difficult to manage disease, your veterinarian may recommend that your pet see a veterinary dermatologist. A board certified veterinary dermatologist has received two to three additional years of training after completing veterinary school, and has successfully completed examinations administered by the American College of Veterinary Dermatology. At the time of this publication, there were approximately 104 of these board certified specialists in the world. Many of them work at a veterinary school, but an increasing number can be found in private practice.

With the proper exercise, veterinary care and nutrition, your dog will exude the benefits of good health and vitality.

Spike may know that his own backyard is a haven for pests that can wreak havoc with this skin and coat.

SPIKE

ABOUT THE SKIN

The skin is the largest organ in the body. It performs a variety of functions to protect and sustain life. These functions include enclosing the body while allowing movement and protecting it from outside environmental influences. The skin needs to be flexible enough to not restrict activity, but tough enough to protect your pet from minor trauma such as scratches and bumps, as well as from irritants and toxins that might otherwise invade the body. In this respect, the skin is much like a wet suit used in water sports.

Protection in the form of pigment deposition in the deeper layers helps to minimize damage by solar radiation. Survival characteristics, such as claw formation used for fighting as well as climbing or digging, are formed in the skin. Temperature regulation is another important function performed in this part of the body. This is controlled through sweat glands and the blood supply. Sweat glands act primarily through evaporation, although they are limited in number and distribution in most pets. The blood vessels in the skin will dilate or widen to allow heat brought by the blood from the core of the body to escape from the surface. Conversely, constriction or narrowing of the vessels help to conserve heat.

Hair is produced in the skin and aids in thermoregulation and physical protection, as

After your pet exercises outdoors, be sure to brush him and check his coat for potentially harmful pests.

well as appearance. Through use of tiny muscles in the skin, the hair shafts can stand erect to allow heat to escape from the surface of the skin, or these shafts may lie down, creating a thin insulating layer of air against the body.

The hair coat provides another layer of protection against trauma. Hairs are deceptively tough as demonstrated by how quickly the blades of scissors or a knife can become dull when cutting hair. Excessive chewing of hair when animals scratch

may actually wear down the teeth. The appearance of an animal with respect to the hair coat is important in socialization, mating, and survival. When your pet's ancestors lived in the wild, the color and pattern of the hair coat acted as camouflage

These two Samoyeds enjoy each other's company on a bright, sunny day, well-protected from highly contagious skin disorders that can affect all members of a household.

This American Staffordshire looks like the King of the Hill with good health and acres to survey.

to protect them from predators, and also allowed them to hunt prey. The same muscles that help regulate body temperature can make the hairs stand erect during confrontation, which is believed to act as non-verbal communication, as well as to make the animal appear larger.

The skin is also an integral part of the immune system, protecting the body from infection by bacteria, fungi, and viruses, as well as helping to prevent the development of tumors. In addition to acting as a physical barrier, there are several types of cells that live in the layers of the skin that act to swallow many of these potentially harmful organisms. Some of these cells are believed to help prevent the formation of some skin tumors by eliminating abnormal cells. The blood vessels also help by bringing other components of the immune system to the skin when needed. Sebum and sweat produced by glands in the skin also contain many ingredients such as immunoglobulins to help fight infection.

Another function of the skin is to provide nerves for sensory perception. These nerves help the individual perceive heat, cold, pain, irritation, and pressure, as well as touch, all of which are necessary for interaction with the environment and for basic survival.

There are different types of glands found in the skin. In addition to the previously mentioned properties of thermoregulation and immune protection, other functions of the glands, include excreting waste material and

Springtime brings beautiful plants and flowers, but also fleas and ticks that can compromise your pet's health.

producing and secreting a variety of substances. For example, the sebaceous glands produce sebum that acts to help keep the skin soft and well-hydrated in addition to its immune defense. Many substances such as fat, protein and electrolytes are stored in the skin. These materials can be easily retrieved when needed by the rest of the body. This organ is also an important source of vitamin D, which is necessary in the regulation of calcium.

Because of the many functions of the skin and its constantly changing or dynamic nature, the skin provides a window into the overall health status of the individual pet. Abnormalities in any part of the process will be revealed in the end result. For example, poor nutrition through poor quality pet food

or an incompletely formulated diet may manifest itself as a dull, brittle, or dry hair coat, poor hair coloration, lusterless skin, dry scaling, or any combination of these characteristics. The skin is a storage organ, and an abnormal appearance or texture may indicate a deficiency of one or more of the nutrients needed by the body.

The level of hydration may also be reflected in the skin. While one of its functions is to protect the body from foreign material or harmful substances, it is very important in preventing the loss of life-sustaining fluid. A pet suffering from dehydration may have skin that feels tacky and does not slide easily over the underlying muscles. Dull or flaky skin may indicate an imbalance of vitamins or essential fatty acids.

Dogs with particularly thick coats, like this Siberian Husky, are particularly susceptible to the skin condition known as "hot spots."

Many deficiencies produce similar changes in the skin, so it is very important to know which specific component is causing the problem. Arbitrary supplementation with nutritional or vitamin supplements may actually cause more harm by creating excessive quantities and/or imbalances of nutrients. The harm may not only be to the skin, but to other organs in the body as well. It is best to have your pet examined by a veterinarian before adding anything to the diet. Generally a good quality, balanced commercial pet food is sufficient for the well-being of the animal. Animals with abnormalities in nutritional requirements or in absorption capabilities may need specific nutritional assistance.

Hair growth is an ongoing process, so changes to the body can be mirrored in this structure. The hair growth cycle is affected by day length, temperature, hormones, nutrition, genetics, illness, and other less definite influences. Changes to any of these factors can alter the cycle and appearance of the hair coat. Many different alterations can produce similar changes in the hair, so again, it is important to ascertain the specific problem. As the skin and hair are constantly changing and growing, it is easy to see how inferior quality or deficiency of the necessary building blocks, (i.e. dietary nutrients), can produce an abnormal appearance and impair the many functions of these structures. Additionally, when the hair coat is compromised for whatever reason—for example, trauma from rubbing,

scratching or hormonal changes—the skin loses some of its protection, and opportunistic infections can develop.

Knowing the structure of the skin helps to explain certain changes in appearance. Basically the skin forms in layers, consisting of the epidermis, (the outermost layer), the dermis, (the supporting layer), and the panniculus, which is essentially the subcutaneous fat. The epidermis itself is subdivided into layers. These layers are not separate entities, but represent different stages in a continual cycle. The basal cell layer, or bottom layer of the epidermis, is where the cells are born. These cells "mature," or keratinize, proceeding to form the outer most layer, the stratum corneum, or horny cell layer.

One way to think of this process is to compare it to the mass production of cookies. The basal cells are like spoonfuls of cookie dough that flatten and harden as they bake, moving on a conveyer belt through the oven, result-

ing in the final product that is stacked more tightly and into a smaller space. The outermost cells normally slough off into the environment. In the normal animal, the speed and degree to which this happens is so subtle that these dead cells are barely noticeable. In certain types of abnormal skin (such as seborrhea) the cycle is accelerated, producing larger sheets of dead cells, seen as white flakes. This change may be due to inflammation, infection, hormonal changes, or a dysfunction of the basal cells.

There is also a significant amount of fluid in all layers of the skin that helps to hold together the outermost cells. With dry skin that can occur in the winter with dry heat indoors, more fluid is lost by evaporation, leading to more cells falling off the surface or flaking. The stratum corneum (horny cell layer) can be likened to a brick wall. The bricks are held together by mortar, a paste-like material with a significant portion that is water. Without the water,

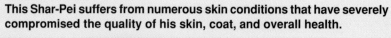
This Shar-Pei suffers from numerous skin conditions that have severely compromised the quality of his skin, coat, and overall health.

Note the drastic contrast in appearance and demeanor in this healthy Shar-Pei.

FOUR MAIN STAGES OF HAIR GROWTH

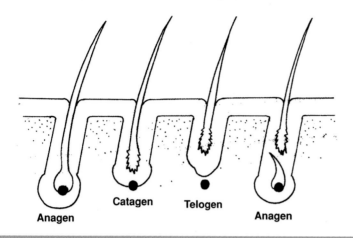

Anagen   Catagen   Telogen   Anagen

This chart offers an illustrated view of the stages of hair growth, any layer of which can be adversely affected by various skin conditions and allergies.

varying degrees, but the timing differs with breeds.

In the normal animal, the individual hair follicles differ slightly from one to another with respect to the particular part of the hair cycle. This prevents bare patches and subsequent loss of protection. Therefore, when the skin can be seen due to the lack of hair in an area that previously had hair, this indicates a disruption in the cycle and warrants investigation of influencing factors.

For example, hairs in the telogen, or resting, phase remain in the follicle, but may be more easily lost by the nature of their attachment in comparison to those in the anagen or growing phase. Therefore, if more hair in one area are in the telogen phase, this area is more likely to have hair loss and subsequent bald patches. This situation can occur by shortening the anagen phase, as occurs in

the mortar is just powder that cannot hold the bricks together. The "mortar" in the skin also contains a large amount of balanced fatty acids. Alteration of this balance (or amount of fatty acids may lead to disruption) of the "brick" wall.

As mentioned, the hair can also demonstrate changes that indicate problems in the body. The hair grows in a cycle consisting essentially of three parts. The *anagen* phase is the active growing phase of the cycle. This phase is followed by the *catagen* phase, that is the time the hair follicle returns to its original form after growth. The last phase is the *telogen* phase that is the resting period of the hair follicle.

These phases will vary in length due to genetic variances between breeds. For example, some dogs have an anagen phase that is relatively short, limiting the length of the hair. These dogs do not need to be clipped and generally the hair falls out, or

sheds, usually on a seasonal basis. Other dogs have a long anagen phase, resulting in long hairs that often are clipped for cosmetic reasons, as well as for ease of care. These hairs are eventually shed as well. All dogs generally grow hair and shed to

The epidermis, dermis and panniculus make up the skin's protective layer, and combine to form the amazing animal you call your pet.

These three playful Labrador Retrievers offer their own demonstration of layers of skin!

illness. The body shifts its energy and nutrients toward fighting the illness and away from growth. The hair bulb, which is where the hair begins, is influenced by a variety of hormones, including gluco–corticosteroids and sex hormones. Any number of imbalances within these substances may lead to alterations in the hair cycle. However, it is im–portant to remember that neu-tering your pet will not create a problem in the hair coat.

The skin is a constantly changing, complex organ that may be affected by numerous external and internal influences. The skin and hair coat often indicates underlying or impending disorders. Its many duties and functions are necessary for the survival of your pet. A well-balanced diet and proper maintenance care in regard to grooming and bathing will help the skin protect your pet and provide him with a healthy, happy life.

Your veterinarian or dermatology specialist is a trusted source for information and treatment programs for your pet's skin and coat health.

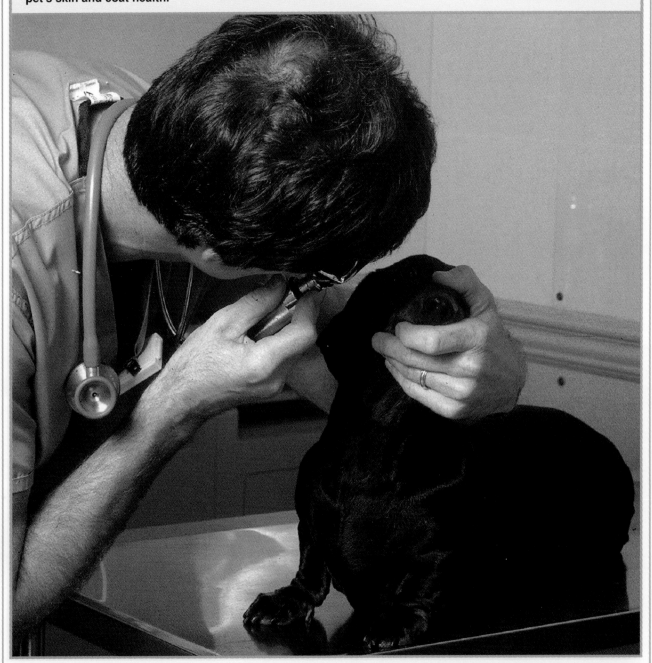

This Redbone named Wray is far more distressed by dangers lurking on the ground than by those on top of skyscrapers!

Besides being well-groomed, this fetching Rottweiler is also particularly well-mannered.

GROOMING AND BATHING

The type and frequency of grooming and bathing will depend greatly on the type of coat your pet has and your expectations concerning your pet's appearance. This chapter is limited to generalizations. More detailed information about grooming specific breeds of dogs is available from your groomer or breed-specific books.

In general, pets without a problem may not require a bath more than several times a year. Pets with skin problems often benefit from baths as often as once a week or more, and from the use of special shampoo. Some pets may have a problem with frequent shampooing, especially using certain shampoos. In some cases, the use of water alone may actually cause irritation. Diseases involving the general health, as well as the skin and hair coat, will also affect grooming decisions. Consultation with your veterinarian or veterinary dermatologist may be necessary.

Under special circumstances, particularly when the condition of the coat is beyond routine bathing, or it is not practical for a pet owner to perform these procedures, a groomer can be your pet's best friend. Professional grooming is also necessary when a certain hair cut or style is desired. Most pets visit a groomer on average every one to four months or so. Professional groomers have undertaken the "hair-raising" task of providing cosmetic care of pets, dealing with the pet owner's expectations, working with sometimes uncooperative animals, and addressing minor skin or ear problems before they get out of control.

They can also be a great asset in providing the proper skin care for a patient suffering from various dermatological problems. A pet owner should become acquatinted with a potential groomer in much the same way they do their veterinarian or family doctor. Young dogs should become accustomed to being bathed and groomed. Please keep in mind that grooming can be very difficult work and a great deal of time may be spent trying to gently take care of mats and other problems. Although most pet owners are appreciative of this, not all pets understand that you and their groomer are working to improve their health and appearance but with time and familiarity, your dog and his groomer can build a great working relationship.

Regular grooming involves more than brushing, bathing, and drying. Conditioning, combing, nail trimming, ear cleaning and in some cases, the expression of anal sacs, are also part of the task. Brushing is probably the most important activity that an owner can perform. Many pets look forward to it as a daily or weekly ritual. Various breeds have vastly different grooming requirements. More frequent brushing for shorter periods of time is better than less

Brushing your dog is a healthy habit that distributes natural, protective oils throughout the pet's skin.

Shampoos and lotions can dry out skin and coat, which can lead to serious health problems. Formulations that include the soothing and anti-bacterial, anti-fungal agent, tea-tree oil are gentle on skin and coat. They're gentle enough to use everyday, yet strong enough to control itching and odors, and to relieve dry skin problems. Photo courtesy of Bonza Pet Care Products.

frequent brushing for longer periods of time.

Frequent brushing will also help to evenly distribute the coat's natural oils, decrease shedding and provide the opportunity to closely evaluate the condition of your pet's skin, hair, ears, nails and feet. It is also a good opportunity to examine the teeth. Members of the household often report that the pet's skin has a bad odor. In reality, a bad odor may be due to the condition of the teeth or gums. Ear problems are often an extension of a skin problem or may be present exclusively. Odors are common with ear infections.

BRUSHING

There are many different types of brushes, some best suited for particular types of hair coats. A slicker brush is available in a variety of sizes and is an excellent general purpose brush for most pets. It usually consists of a rectangular head with fine, close metal bristles that may be bent or somewhat resemble a "bed of nails." If used gently, it is a wonderful tool.

To use it, the hair is parted and then brushed out from the skin in layers. This action helps prevent and loosen mats and remove the undercoat of hair. It is very important to be gentle and not damage or hurt the skin. Having a professional groomer perform an initial grooming and brushing is a great way to get started. They may also be able to help by selecting the correct type of brush to use and providing instruction on how to use it.

Frequent brushing helps prevent mats, but they may still occur. Mats should be handled very cautiously. Often they can be worked out with the use of a dematting spray or powder, and by using the fingers to pull the mat into smaller pieces. A similar technique may be used with burrs or grass awns. If your attemps at mat removal cause too much discomfort, it is probably better to clip out the mat. Electric clippers are better than scissors because scissors may cut the underlying skin. The removal of mats may reveal a problem that actually caused the formation of mats. Medical attention may be necessary in some severe cases.

BATHING

Selecting the proper shampoo for your pet can be a daunting task. An all-

Be especially careful to avoid the eye area when shampooing your pet.

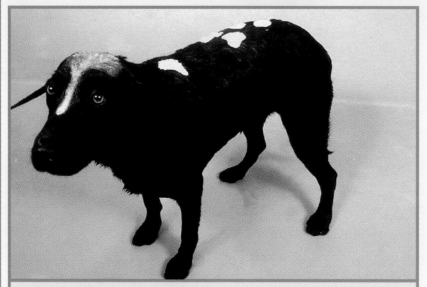

Your groomer or veterinarian can offer guidance concerning the appropriate shampoo or treatment for your dog. Photo courtesy of Dr. Tom Manning.

also important to note that shampoos are seldom a "cure all." When the correct shampoo is utilized in an appropriate manner, it can be of significant benefit. However, in many situations, shampoo therapy alone may not be enough.

Medicated shampoos may be utilized as a part of a maintenance program for a pet diagnosed as having a certain dermatological condition. Medicated shampoos may also be used as a means of controlling a problem, or while waiting for the results of medical tests.

With chronic conditions, it is important to try to have a

natural shampoo is not necessarily a better shampoo. Individual preference, your pet's type of coat, and his skin condition will dictate which shampoo is best for each bath. In most cases, a mild shampoo may be all that is required. The coat should be thoroughly rinsed afterwards. A conditioner may then be beneficial in some breeds. In certain situations, a medicated shampoo may be necessary.

The type of medicated shampoo you should use depends on the type of skin problem that is present. Some shampoos are best used to help control bacterial skin infections, while others are better at controlling a specific condition, such as seborrhea.

Your pet's shampoo requirements will likely change over time. A shampoo that is appropriate when one dermatological condition is present may not be appropriate at another time. It is

The beach is a marvelous place to exercise your dog, but even sand and sea can harbor potential dangers to your pet's skin.

If you can eliminate the tugging and tearing of your dog's coat in the detangling process, your dog will appreciate it, and his coat is less likely to be split or torn. Photo courtesy of Wahl, USA.

liquid) to help speed the recovery and more quickly improve the quality of the hair and skin.

Four of the more common types of ingredients in anti-microbial shampoos include chlorhexidine, ethyl lactate, benzoyl peroxide and iodine. Iodine is actually seldom used anymore because of its potential problems, including staining, irritation and allergic reaction. Chlorhexidine and ethyl lactate are usually well-tolerated and effective. Benzoyl peroxide may be found alone or in combination with other ingredients. It is quite effective and helps decrease "greasiness," but

confirmed diagnosis of what is causing the skin problem. Various diagnostic tests may be recommended by your veterinarian or veterinary dermatologist as part of a plan to identify and treat your pet's skin condition. Without a confirmed diagnosis, it may not be possible to determine which is the best shampoo to use. In some cases, shampoo and even water alone may cause greater irritation. It is possible that the best shampoo available may not be appropriate or adequate. Additional types of therapy (pills or injections) may be necessary.

Anti-microbial shampoos help control bacterial and fungal infections. They may be used as a sole treatment in mild infections or to prevent the infections from coming back. With more involved infections, they may be used in conjunction with oral medications (pills or

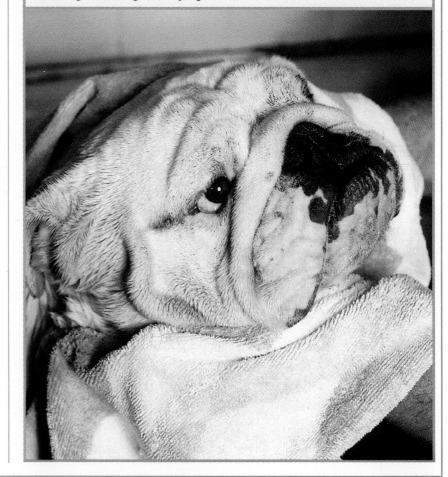

Pets with wrinkled skin like this Bulldog are in need of particularly thorough washing and drying.

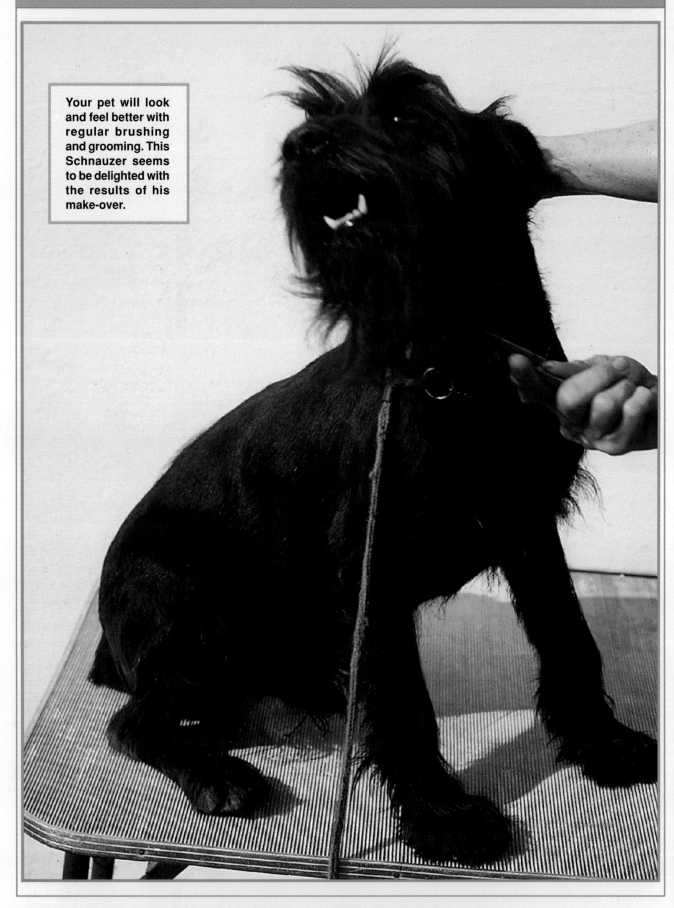

Your pet will look and feel better with regular brushing and grooming. This Schnauzer seems to be delighted with the results of his make-over.

can be irritating. All of the above ingredients fight bacteria, but only the chlorhexidine and iodine have properties that fight fungi (and yeast). Recently, new shampoos have been released that have better activity against yeast organisms.

Anti-seborrhea shampoos may be used to help control conditions ranging from dry scales or flakes (dandruff) to a greasy and oily hair coat. Shampoo therapy is an indispensable part of therapy for a pet suffering from primary seborrhea. It is also an extremely important factor in controlling secondary seborrhea until the underlying reason can be diagnosed and treated. Anti-seborrhea shampoos help decrease scales, or dandruff, by either decreasing scale formation or speeding its removal from the skin and coat. Examples of ingredients that can help with this problem include tar, sulfur and salicylic acid. Benzoyl peroxide helps decrease greasiness and speed removal of scales and flakes but can also be drying or irritating. Often two or more of these ingredients may be combined into one product to improve efficacy. The use of generic products should be avoided because quality control and the correct mixture of ingredients is necessary to obtain the best results.

Often these anti-seborrhea shampoos do not provide what we would expect in lathering action. However, this does not mean that they are not effective in their intended purpose. It may be beneficial to bathe your pet with a general cleansing shampoo before using any medicated shampoo.

Although flea shampoos are helpful in short-term flea control, they do not provide long lasting protection. The adult fleas seen on a pet actually account for approximately 10% or less of the total flea population. Significant number of eggs, larvae, and pre-adult fleas remain in the environment. There are much more effective means of dealing with and preventing a flea problem that are discussed later in this book.

Shampoos can also help decrease itching. They work in two ways: They treat disease and infections that contribute to itching, or they may be soothing and help reduce the itching itself. For small localized areas, sprays, lotions and creams are appropriate. For larger areas, shampoos may be necessary. Colloidal oatmeal can be found in virtually all forms of topical therapy. In some cases, it is very beneficial, but its length of action

Oatmeal has been used for centuries to relieve itchy skin, and now you can find it as an ingredient in shampoos for your dog to help soothe his scratching and cleanse his skin. Photo courtesy of Francodex.

Dogs with unusual coats, like this corded Komondor, may need special shampoos.

is usually less than two days.

Topical antihistamines may be found alone or in combination with other ingredients. They have not been shown to have a beneficial effect, and with prolonged use, may result in contact reactions. Because of this and the additional cost associated with products containing antihistamines, veterinary dermatologists seldom recommend them.

Topical anesthetics generally offer a very short duration of effect, and in some cases, can even cause contact reactions. Other topical medications may provide very short-term relief but seldom are appropriate for long-term control of itching.

Topical steroids are probably the most useful topical medications. However, they are not without risks. If used excessively, they can cause localized and systemic side effects. Some topical steroid medications also contain other ingredients, such as alcohol, that can irritate the skin.

In some animals, the application of any substance, including water, can result in an increased level of irritation. Your pet's skin condition and shampoo needs will likely change with time and response to therapy. Inappropriate use of medications can worsen a skin problem and delay the initiation of appropriate therapy. Your veterinarian or veterinary dermatologist can help recommend which topical medications should be used to best improve the quality of your pet's skin and hair coat.

A well-groomed dog is a happier dog, so don't let cumbersome grooming tools stop you from getting the job done. There are compact, lightweight tools available. Photo courtesy of Wahl, USA.

To keep the long, silky locks of the Lhasa Apso in top form, the dog himself must be in top form—as these two are.

While it is highly recommended to include your pet in vacation plans, remember to always check his coat for fleas and ticks—especially in wooded areas.

FIGHTING FLEAS, TICKS AND OTHER PARASITES

FLEAS

Many people are under the false impression that if fleas or flea bites do not affect humans, fleas are not a problem for their pet. Most fleas prefer dogs and cats to humans. Mild to moderate flea infestations may not actually result in a problem for humans in the house, but a relatively few number of fleas can cause a significant problem for the animals in the house. Devices called "flea traps" are extremely useful for illustrating the presence of fleas in the indoor environment and emphasizing the need for environmental control of fleas. Unfortunately, they are not effective as a sole means of eliminating fleas in the house. Consultation with a veterinarian concerning potential toxicities and effectiveness is strongly recommended when implementing any flea control program.

Flea control can be an extremely frustrating process, but success can be achieved with an organized approach to the problem. Some basic information concerning fleas is useful in addressing the solution. The cat flea is by far the most common flea to infest both dogs and cats in the US. While other types of fleas may occur, treatment using the biology of the cat flea will generally treat most other types as well. Flea eggs are white and quite small, approximately 0.5 millimeters in length. Depending on temperature and humidity, these eggs can hatch from one to ten days after being deposited by the female. While the eggs are deposited on the pet, they do not stick to the body or hair, and quickly fall off into the immediate environment. The larvae that hatch are between 2 to 5 millimeters

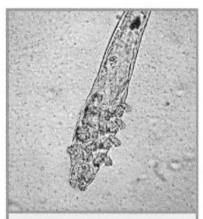

The Demodex mite is passed from the dam to her puppies. It affects youngsters from the ages of three to ten months.

in length and are worm-like organisms that feed on organic debris and flea feces. They avoid light and move deep into the carpet or under grass, leaves, or soil.

Larvae are very sensitive to heat and desiccation. This sensitivity, in addition to the nutritional requirement of adult flea feces, allows the larvae to thrive only in selected areas where the pet spends much of his time. These areas include shaded, moist ground and the carpet or spaces in hardwood floors. Once the larvae are completely developed, they produce a cocoon in which they mature into adult fleas. Prior to emerging from this cocoon, the adults are in their most protected state. Inside, they are resistant to drying out, and to insecticides. This stage can protect the adult for up to 140 days until the right stimulus occurs to induce the emergence from the cocoon. This can be physical pressure, heat, or carbon dioxide. (Vibration has been considered to be a factor as well, but this has not yet been proven by research). The variable length of this stage helps ensure survival when conditions are optimal. It is the shortest under ideal conditions, often found in the home, and can lead to a life cycle of only 2 to 4 weeks.

After emergence, the adult flea is attracted to light and avoids deeper carpet or vegetation in an effort to be closer to a passing animal. Contrary to previous belief, the flea spends the majority of its time on the pet. They generally live for only a matter of days when off your pet's body. Fleas are attracted to the pet by body heat, carbon dioxide, and movement, and move primarily only when stimulated. The female flea first requires a meal, which is blood from biting your pet, in order to begin producing eggs. These females are capable of producing several thousand eggs in their lifetime. To make this many eggs, a large amount of food, (i.e. blood), is necessary. This is evident by the life-threatening anemia that can occur in animals with a heavy infestation of fleas. Male fleas feed as well but to a lesser degree. While feeding, fleas excrete digested blood that appears as pepper-like material known as flea dirt. Occasionally, this is mistakenly identified as eggs. Flea dirt will color water red, indicating the original source as blood.

With this basic knowledge, treatment for fleas can be adjusted to provide the most complete control. While fleas do spend most of their time on the pet, control is still essentially a three-pronged attack, targeting the yard, house, and pet. It is impor-tant to remember that wild animals and stray animals can be a continuing source of fleas in the yard as well as in crawl spaces and attics. Also, bearing in mind the adaptive length of the cocoon phase of the flea's life cycle, a sudden increase in fleas in the home after a vacation may not be from the boarding facility where your pet was staying, but rather a result of the stimulation of the emerging adult fleas upon your return.

This is an exciting time for flea control, with many new advances in products based on the discovery of aspects of the flea's biology. Killing the biting and breeding adult flea is certainly one important part of the process. Equally important is preventing fleas from becoming adult fleas. This second part of this process is performed with a group of compounds called insect growth regulators that block the development of the immature stages.

More recently, agents have been developed to damage or kill the many eggs and the larvae as well. In the yard, a spray to kill adult fleas can be used every two weeks for several treatments during the prime flea season to eliminate the emerging adult fleas. The addition of an insect growth regulator enhances the effec-tiveness and provides greater long-term control. Many of these products can be broken down by sunlight, so finding an agent designed for use in the yard is necessary.

It is always important to follow all the precautions on the spray's label to avoid toxic reactions for you and your pet and to avoid run-off into lakes and streams. Concentrate

Some veterinarians recommend bathing your dog after he's been swimming in a lake or the ocean because bacteria and other parasites may be present in the water.

your efforts in areas where your pet spends most of his time, remembering the types of environments the flea prefers.

In the home, a similar plan is also used. Vacuuming the house and disposing of the bag outdoors is an important first step. Wash the pet's bedding in hot water. Again, when treating the home, use a product that kills both adults and immature fleas and blocks the ongoing life cycle. By blocking the continuation of the life cycle, treatment of the home can be performed less frequently. Because of the nature of flea development, concentrate your treatments in the areas where your pet stays most often, but be sure to treat the entire house, including closets, attics, basements, porches, and crawl spaces. Make sure a spray is used under furniture, even after the use of foggers. If foggers are used, one is needed for every room, including hallways, as the fog will not go around corners.

Bearing in mind the short life cycle under ideal conditions, (i.e. inside the house), the treatments need to be spaced two weeks apart in heavy infestations. Maintenance treatment can be months apart with the proper product. Again, follow all safety precautions on the labels of all materials used, and protect all pets from exposure, including fish tanks and bird cages.

Products for use on your pet have made the most significant recent advances.

The deer tick is the most common carrier of Lyme Disease.

Shampoos can be used weekly but some products can be drying and most have a very short duration of effectiveness. Dips may last longer but cannot be used as often due to potential toxicity when combined with some products. Powders and spot-on products are available also. There are also numerous sprays and foams on the market, most of which kill adult fleas and vary in the duration of action on the pet. The length of time these products work varies depending on the formulation of the product, environmental conditions, and degree of flea infestation. Flea collars exist in a wide range of types with a large variation in reported effectiveness.

Shampoos and sprays can be effective and useful first steps in addressing a flea problem. Some of the newer products state that they are effective in damaging the flea eggs before and after falling off the pet's body. This would

A diet that includes pure lamb protein and wholesome grains can give your dog the ingredients he needs for overall good health—a condition that's reflected in supple skin and a lustrous, full coat. Photo courtesy of Nature's Recipe Pet Foods.

be helpful in breaking the continuing cycle. One product in the form of a monthly pill effects the development of the flea by entering the egg while it is in the female flea, essentially preventing the development of new fleas.

The newest on-pet products are designed to last several weeks and come in a spray or liquid that is placed on the pet's neck or back and spreads over the body. These products are designed to kill the adults before they bite, preventing the production of eggs as well as the reaction to the flea bite. The duration and effectiveness of these materials may be affected by frequency of bathing and the condition of the skin. Repellents in the form of different fragrances are thought to be useful in preventing the flea from feeding and subsequent egg production. Many products on the market have success rates that vary with individuals and have not been extensively researched through scientific study. Which product to use on your pet depends on individual environments, type of pet, and your ability to perform the necessary tasks, as well as exposure to new areas with fleas and re-introduction of fleas into a treated area.

TICKS

Ticks are another type of insect that may feed on the blood of your pet. They can be a source of infection by certain parasites, viruses, fungi, bacteria, and other pathogenic organisms that cause such diseases as Rocky Mountain Spotted Fever and Lyme disease. There are four stages of the life cycle of the most common classification of ticks. In addition to the egg and the adult, there is a larval stage and a nymph stage, both of which must feed completely before detaching from the pet and molting to the next stage. The adult may increase its weight 100 times while feeding and can produce thousands of eggs after detachment. There is a risk of life-threatening anemia with massive tick infestation. The greatest risk of infection from the diseases that may be carried by ticks is when the tick is infected at the youngest possible stages such as the egg or larva. The disease is passed to subsequent

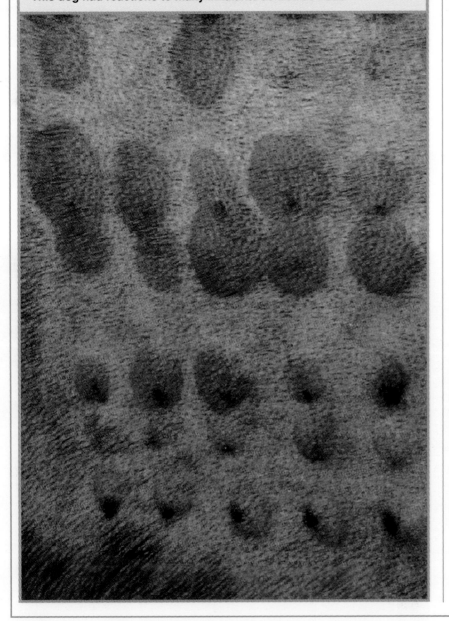

Intradermal allergy testing is very important to the diagnostic process. This dog had reactions to many inhalants as well as fleas.

stages, all of which feed on the host, increasing the chance of transmitting the disease to your pet. The saliva from ticks, in addition to the unusual possibility of causing severe whole-body disease, can affect the body's immune system at that site, allowing infection to occur. The bite itself is painless, allowing the tick to stay attached and undetected by its host. This time frame allows for feeding as well as the transmission of any disease the tick is carrying. In some instances, the bite's site can become irritated by the local infection or a reaction to the mouth parts of the tick, causing the pet to repeatedly scratch at the area.

Ticks are attracted by motion, heat, carbon dioxide, and changes in light. They do not jump or fly and rely on direct contact to get onto the pet. Therefore avoidance is the best method of preventing tick problems. Should a tick attach to your pet's skin, prompt removal is required. This may be done with fine-pointed tweezers or any number of tick removal devices that get as close as possible to the skin surface and gently pull the tick free. The types of ticks with strong mouth parts may take a tiny piece of skin with removal and the ones with fragile mouth parts may leave fragments of these parts behind. Both situations may cause localized irritation. The area should be cleaned with soap

and water to prevent infection. The person removing the tick should wear gloves and avoid contact with the insect. Petroleum jelly, matches, and other such home remedies are not effective and may make the situation worse. Ticks may be killed with any number of the flea products discussed previously and the label on each will reveal its effectiveness. Environmental control may be achieved on a limited basis through sprays. Elimination of other hosts, such as deer and rodents, has not been successful in controlling ticks. There is one tick collar on the market that prevents the attachment of ticks and induces detachment of any ticks present within a time period to minimize transmission of disease.

It is advisable to gently shampoo your dog as certain skin conditions are easily irritated with any form of intervention.

Internal parasites can cause skin problems, which is why it's important to keep your pet parasite-free—like this Afghan Hound puppy.

This dog exhibited facial and oral sores associated with a severe type of the autoimmune disease, Pemphigus. Photo courtesy of Dr. Diane Bevier, Heska Corporation, Fort Collins, Co.

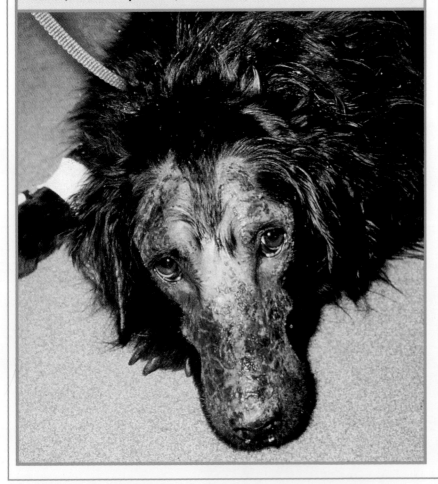

INTERNAL PARASITES

Internal parasites do not normally cause problems in the skin. If they do, it is by affecting your pet's overall health. They may make a pet more susceptible to skin infections, or may affect the normal healthy biology of the skin. In some cases, these internal parasites may find their way to the skin and cause sores, rashes or itching. If a patient has heartworms and/or intestinal parasites in addition to skin problems, various test results may be effected. For both general health reasons and to get a clearer picture of what is causing a skin problem, it is advisable to test for and treat for these internal parasites if they are present.

MITES AND MANGE

Most mites are so small that their presence can only be confirmed through the use of a microscope. The two most common mites seen in dogs are demodex and sarcoptic mites. Dogs exhibiting disease associated with either of these mites is said to have "mange." Other mites such as cheyletiella, ear mites and other less common mites can also be associated with skin problems.

An infestation with sarcoptic mites, also called scabies mange, is one of the most itchy diseases seen in dogs. It is potentially highly contagious, but not all animals that are exposed to the affected pet will become affected themselves. Some dogs may actually harbor the mites on their bodies, but not show any symptoms.

Since your dog is not able to tell you that he has fleas, look for signs like excessive itching and scratching.

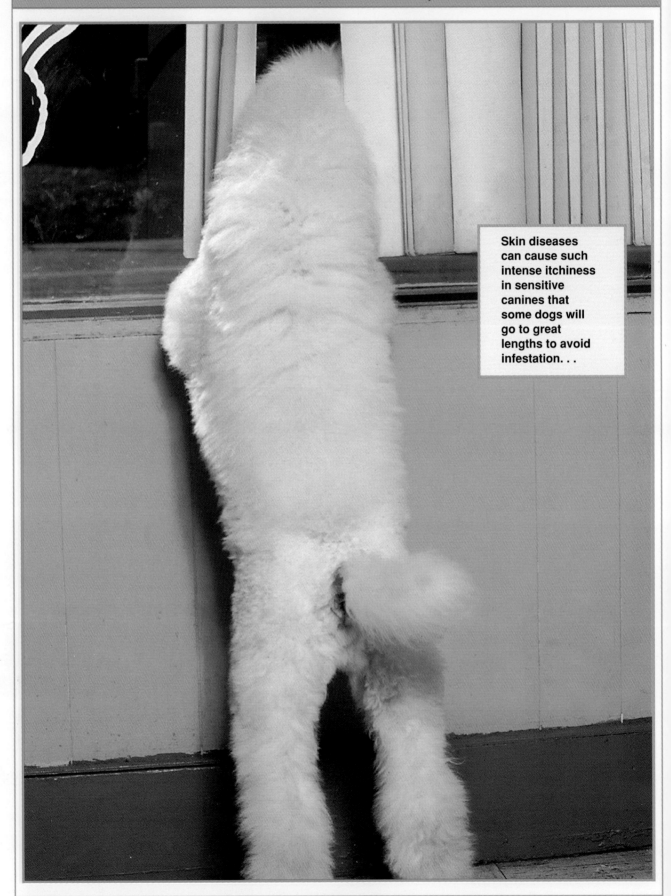

Skin diseases can cause such intense itchiness in sensitive canines that some dogs will go to great lengths to avoid infestation. . .

. . .or great depths, as the case may be.

Typical clinical signs include extreme itching and crusts on the margins of the ear, elbows, and skin over the breast bone. However, some animals will be affected in different areas or may only show signs of itching without any crusts, redness or hair loss. The mites have also been known to temporarily cause problems in humans. If you suspect this, you are advised to seek an evaluation by a dermatologist.

The human scabies mite is different than the dog scabies mite and is generally believed not to be transmissible from humans to dogs. Microscopic diagnosis of scabies mange can be difficult to confirm because of the small number of mites required to cause clinical signs. Often, response to appropriate therapy is the method used to make the diagnosis of this mite infesta-tion. Treatment may consist of various topical sponge-on "dips" to the "extralable use" of Ivermectin. Dips actually refer to the sponged-on application of diluted anti-parisitic medications that are not rinsed off after use. They are effective in many cases, but may be unpleasant and tedious to apply, and require repeated applications.

Although the potential side effects of ivermectin can be life threatening, it is often the therapy of choice in treating an infestation with scabies mites. With either drug, all pets that have come into contact with the infected dog should be treated. Due to breed-associated problems (possible coma and death) with Ivermectin, it should only be used with caution and not in every situation.

Demodex mites usually do not cause itching, but can in some cases. These mites are actually found on uninfected dogs and are not considered contagious. Transmission of mites occurs when puppies are a few days old and nurs-ing.

Occasionally, dogs may show clinical signs associated with the presence of these mites such as patchy hair loss on the face and feet, unac-companied by itching. Some-times other areas of the body are affected and itching may be present. Mild cases affect-ing a single or a few limited areas of skin are referred to as having localized demodicosis. More severe cases that affect several areas or even the whole body are referred to as having general-ized demodicosis.

Genetic predisposition, general ill health and the use of drugs that supress the immune system, such as steroids, can contribute to generalized demodicosis. The most severe cases are often infected with bacteria and the skin may resemble severe acne in humans. Open sores may ooze and have a foul odor. The diagnosis is con-firmed by microscopic exami-nation of samples scraped from the skin.

Localized demodicosis is self-limiting and will often go away on its own. This is most common type of demodicosis seen in young dogs. General-ized demodicosis is treated differently than the localized disease and is considered to have a genetic basis. There-fore, dogs that have had generalized demodicosis should not be bred because they may pass on the ten-

This dachshund suffered from a very rare disease involving the death of the cells in the epidermal layer of the skin. Notice the afflicted toes pic–tured here.

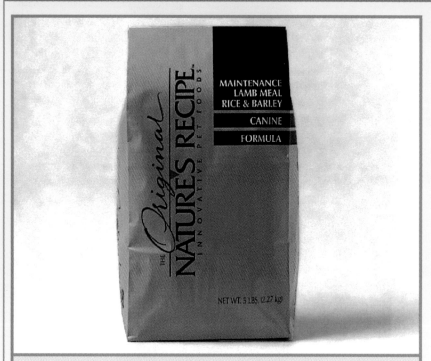

To keep your dog looking his best, you need to feed him a food that is high in digestibility, one that contains the highest quality ingredients. Photo courtesy of Nature's Recipe Pet Foods.

dency for aquiring this disease to future generations. Treatment of a localized case of demodicosis with the same regimen used to treat a generalized case of demodicosis may artificially prevent an animal from developing the symptoms of a genetic disease. This could result in inadvertently passing on the tendency for this disease to future generations.

It is important to note that while generalized demodicosis may initially appear similar to a localized demodicosis, the vast majority of localized cases do not progress to the more severe form and therefore do not have the genetic predilection for the generalized disease. It is imperative that we do our best to prevent the breeding of dogs that harbor the genetic predilection for generalized demodicosis.

Before the development of the drug Amatraz, many dogs with this diease were put to sleep. This sponge-on "dip" is thoroughly applied weekly or bi-weekly after a bath. It is important not to bathe a patient between dips. Although treatment failures occur, they are rare. The most common reason for failure is lack of follow-up veterinary visits and discontinuing the dips before the disease is completely cured. It is not uncommon for a dog to exhibit dramatic improvement, but still harbor these mites. I routinely recommend continuing the dips on a biweekly or weekly basis for at least three to four weeks after a patient has had several negative skin scrapes. In some cases, reevaluation and skin scrapes are also recommended one month after discontinuing treatment. If a

patient fails to respond to Amatraz, the frequency of application or concentration of the dip solution may be increased. This may increase the possiblity of side effects. If Amatraz is not effective or recurrance of the disease occurs, the daily use of ivermectin may be considered. As discussed elsewhere, this drug can have devistating and life-threatening side effects, but it can also save the the life of a pet severly affected with demodectic mange.

LICE

The diagnosis of lice in small animals is becoming increasingly rare. This is due in part to the use of flea control products that usually are very effective in eliminating lice. These parasites, unlike mites, are large enough that they or their eggs are usually visible to the naked eye. The type of louse that affects humans is different than the type of louse that affects dogs, which is also different than the type of louse that effects cats. In other words, these different types of lice only affect a specific type of animal. Lice can cause inflamation of the skin and profound itching, but are usually easily treated with many products used to kill fleas.

OTHER PARASITES

A variety of other parasites ranging from cheyletiella to mosquitoes can cause skin problems in animals. Most common parasitic problems are relatively easily diagnosed and treated. In many cases, they can complicate the dignosis and treatment of other skin problems.

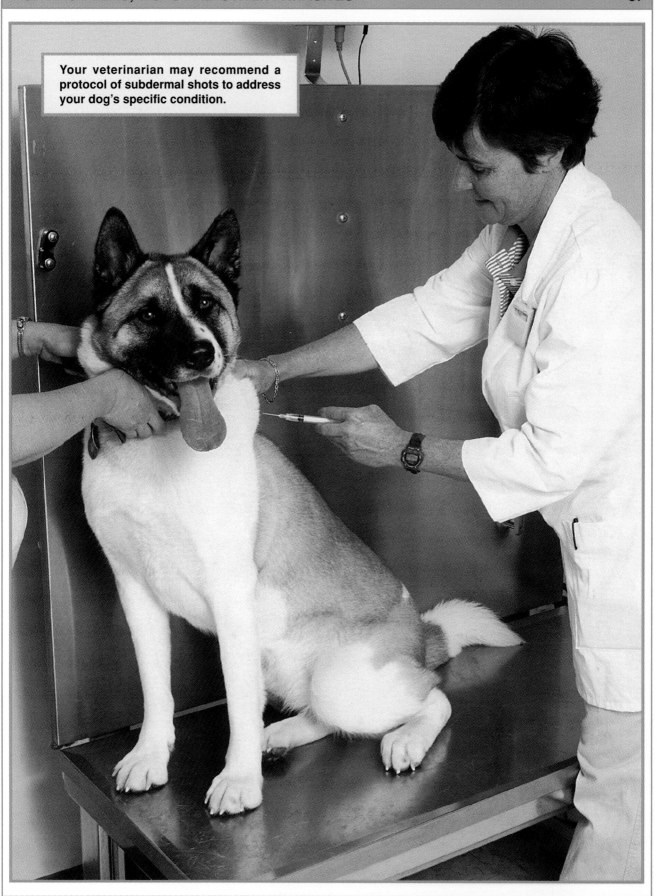

Your veterinarian may recommend a protocol of subdermal shots to address your dog's specific condition.

Intradermal testing can precisely pinpoint the culprits in your dog's environment that trigger his allergic conditions.

ALLERGIES

The two most common types of allergies seen in dogs include flea allergy and inhalant allergy (similar to hay fever in humans). Food allergy is much more rare. Contact allergy is significantly less common than food allergy. Often these different types of allergies may have symptoms that look alike with only subtle differences in history, distribution of clinical signs, or response to therapy. The hallmark clinical sign of allergies is itching. However, some allergic pets may manifest the disease in other ways, such as ear or skin infections. The basic physiological aspect of the different types of allergies is similar. The allergy-causing substance gains entrance into the body either through the skin, lungs or digestive tract. In normal animals, these substances (called allergens) do not cause the individual any problems. In affected animals, the allergens cause an abnormal immune response resulting in various clinical signs. These clinical signs will be discussed individually with each allergy.

FLEA ALLERGY

Flea allergy is the most common allergy seen in dogs and it is one of the most itchy diseases encountered. A majority of flea-allergic dogs will also suffer from inhalant allergies. In contrast to a non-flea-allergic dog that itches when exposed to several fleas, a flea-allergic dog can suffer from extreme discomfort associated with a single flea. The flea allergy reaction occurs when a flea bites a flea-allergic dog and exposes the dog's immune system to flea saliva. The ensuing allergic reaction can occur very quickly, and may also last for many days. Clinical signs are often more severe near the area of the flea bite, but can also occur in distant locations. Itching, redness, small bumps and self-induced trauma from scratching result. As with flea infestation, the most severely affected area is often on or near the "rump" region, where flea numbers are usually at their greatest. Excessive licking or chewing of both the front and rear legs and paws can be seen with flea allergy as well as other allergies.

Eradication of fleas is the most important aspect of controlling a flea-allergic dog. Flea control measures that kill fleas by requiring them to be exposed to a toxin only after biting the dog and ingesting the dog's blood are

Scratching is known to exacerbate an allergic reaction, and may even lead to further infections. This Boxer is trying to rid himself of fleas.

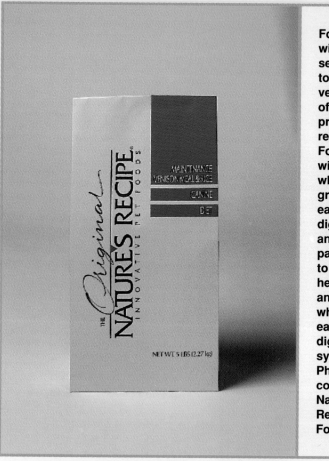

For dogs with dietary sensitivities to the meats, venison often provides relief. Formulated with wholesome grains for easy digestibility and palatability to nourish healthy skin and coat while being easy on the digestive system. Photo courtesy of Nature's Recipe Pet Foods.

Every part of the body can be adversely affected by the onset of allergies. Fortunately, this Shih Tzu is beautiful all over.

not very helpful in treating a flea-allergic dog in the short term. They may help reduce the total number of fleas. However, before the flea dies, they must bite the pet, thus initiating the allergic reaction. Flea shampoos are also not very helpful because they do not offer significant residual repellent action. The shampoo kills the fleas on the pet, but fleas from the environment quickly jump back on and the itching continues.

Environmental control, the use of insect growth regulating hormones, and topical application of products with residual action are imperative components of stringent flea control for a flea-allergic dog. Consultation with a veterinarian concerning potential toxicities and effectiveness is strongly recommended when implementing any flea control program.

ALLERGEN INHALANT DERMATITIS

Allergic inhalant dermatitis is also called *atopy*. This disease involves allergic reactions to various pollens or spores from grasses, trees, molds, and weeds, as well as other substances with microscopic allergens that can be inhaled such as dust and dust mites. These substances interact with the dog's immune system primarily through the lungs. Absorption through the skin is also a factor. Humans with inhalant allergies primarily suffer from symptoms such as runny noses, irritated eyes, and sneezing. Dogs manifest this type of allergy by scratching, rubbing, licking, and biting themselves. The feet, forearms, armpits, abdominal

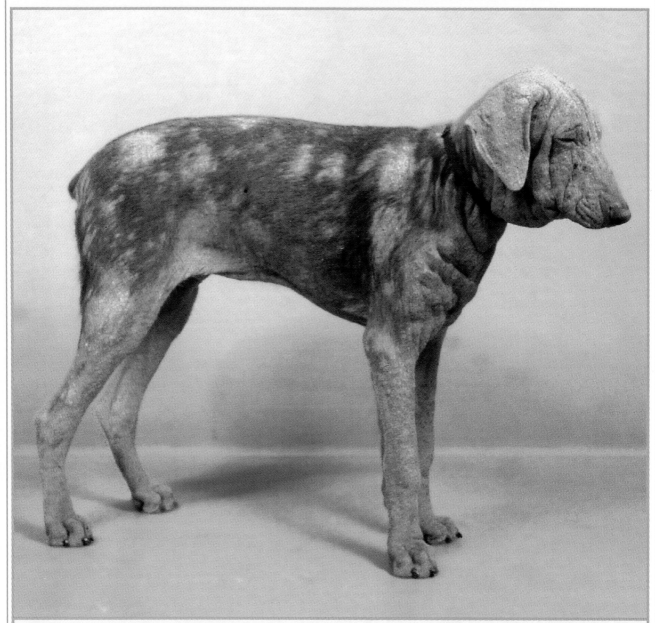

Above: This Doberman has a case of generalized demodicosis with a secondary bacterial infection. **Below**: A close-up view of the bacterial infection.

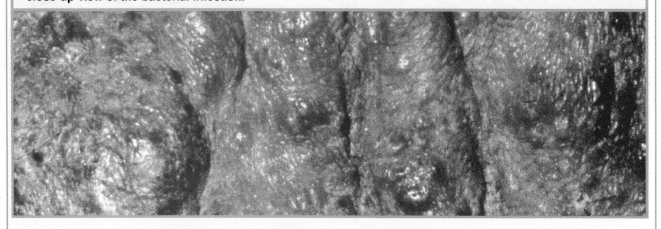

region, face, ears and occasionally the rump may become red and irritated.

Many dogs may only be affected in one or two of these areas. Some dogs may seem to itch all over their body. Ear and skin infections and body odor are also often noted. Some pet's itching may not be as obvious, but they may still have ear problems associated with allergies. The symptoms often start sometime between the age of one to three years and initially cause problems during a particular season. With time, the clinical signs become more severe and may last all year long. In mild climates, the symptoms may initially start at a younger age and be present year round. Bacterial and yeast infections take advantage of the abnormal skin and are often a secondary problem.

Although controlling exposure to the allergens that cause flea, food and contact allergy may be possible, it is very difficult to control exposure to substances in the air. If the clinical signs cause the pet to be uncomfortable, medical therapy may be necessary. Allergy testing should be considered if the symptoms do not adequately respond to medical therapy; if side effects of the drugs occur; if the expense of the drugs is too great; or if the necessary frequency of medication administration is cumbersome.

Currently, two different methods for allergy testing exist. Skin testing for allergies involves the intradermal injection of small amounts of various types of diluted purified allergen extracts and monitoring for a wheal (a localized reaction that looks like a "hive" or "welt").

Skin testing, or intradermal skin testing as it is also known, is similar to the allergy test that most people are familiar with, that is used for allergy testing humans. Blood testing is a relatively new type of test that involves obtaining a sample of blood and submitting it to a laboratory that performs the specialized testing. After the positive reactions identified with the allergy test are correlated with the history, the immunotherapy solution (allergy extract) can be formulated.

An overall view of a Cocker Spaniel who suffered from acute itching. This case demonstrates the need for diagnostic testing, because common symptoms may appear in a variety of disorders.

Dogs can be allergic to many different things—including simple tap water. Fortunately, this Golden's coat and ears are always treated after a swim.

This solution contains a mixture of specific allergens. The exact mix of allergens is different for each patient and is based upon the pet's history, positive allergy test results, the veterinarian's (and/or the laboratory's) clinical experience in treating allergies and other considerations. Injections of immunotherapy solution or allergy extract are also referred to as "allergy shots." (This type of "allergy shot" should not be confused with steroid or cortisone injections, which are quite different).

The treatment of allergies is complicated, and the likelihood of success with immuno-therapy (or allergy shots) can be affected by a number of factors. The allergy tests themselves can be technically complicated and are best interpreted by a veterinarian with specialized training in the treatment of allergic skin diseases. The most precise results are obtained with the use of individual allergens rather than groups of aller-gens. The disadvantage of using groups of mixed aller-gens becomes apparent when considering the results of the test. When a group of mixed allergens has a negative test, all allergens in the group or mix are considered to be negative. This is unfortunate because if the allergens were tested individually, one of the allergens could actually show a true positive test result. Con-versely, a group of mixed allergens that test positive may actually contain a individual allergen that would truly test negative if individual testing were performed.

The less accurate nature of using groups or mixes for allergy testing complicates the formulation of the immunotherapy solution and may inadvertently lead to omission of an important allergen in the allergy extract. Additionally, the practice of using groups or mixes could lead to the inclusion of allergens that are not relevant, thereby diluting the concentration of the important allergens. Both situations are likely to reduce the efficacy of the treatment.

Studies indicate that the highest success rate with immunotherapy is achieved through the use of the most precise testing and the highest concentration of immunotherapy solution. Grouping of allergens should be avoided in either type of allergy test and eventually the highest concentration of immunotherapy solution that can safely be used should be administered as an immunotherapy injection or "allergy shot."

An additional complicating factor in testing for allergies is the presence of two different immunoglobulins (products of the immune system) which are important in allergies and allergy testing. These immunoglobulins are known as IgE and IgGd. IgE is found both in the blood stream and the skin. IgGd is found only in the skin. Tests that rely solely on measuring blood levels of IgE have an inherent disadvantage when compared to other tests that utilize both IgGd and IgE (blood and skin levels) as indicators of allergies. Some falsely negative allergy tests may be seen when blood allergy tests are performed on animals that have normal levels of IgE in their blood but still itch because of allergies associated with the IgGd or IgE found in the skin.

Skin testing, or intradermal skin testing, allows for relatively inexpensive identification of individual allergens and is able to take into account skin levels of both of the important allergy associated immunoglobulins (IgE and IgGd). It also has the advantage of actually testing the skin which is the "organ" of the body that is affected by the allergic disease. Commercial blood tests for allergies measure only blood IgE and do not measure the immunoglobulins found in the skin (IgGd and skin bound IgE). Although it is possible to utilize groups or mixes of allergens with skin testing, most allergens are tested for individually.

The concentration of the immunotherapy (allergy extract) solution can also vary with the type of test performed and as previously discussed can affect the success rate. Skin testing has numerous advantages over blood testing, but is complicated to perform and interpret. Both types of tests are best performed under the guidance of a veterinarian with training in allergic skin diseases.

If a pet is diagnosed as having allergic inhalant dermatitis, there are several different methods of therapy. The first is to remove the offending allergen from the animal's environment. Unfortunately, this is not possible in most instances. The second method involves the use of drugs or medications. In general, an adequate response to medical therapy, not including steroids, is noted in approximately 20-30% of patients with allergic inhalant dermatitis. Each pet is different and different regions of the country and the word will likely exhibit different response rates. Various types of medications and combinations may be tried until the best one is determined.

Many skin problems are the result of food allergies, which can be minimized by careful analysis of and attention to the ingredients in your dog's diet. High-quality ingredients typically result in fewer problems. Photo courtesy of Nature's Recipe Pet Foods.

It is oftentimes easier to see fleas and ticks on lighter-coated dogs than their darker contemporaries.

In medium to large breed dogs, the cost of medications would likely be more than the cost of immunotherapy injections based on allergy testing. However, medications usually result in relatively quick improvement, while immunotherapy injections may take three to twelve months or more until improvement is noted.

Immunotherapy injections (hyposensitization or "allergy shots") consists of series of diluted allergens that are given by subcutanous (under the skin) injections to change a pet's immune system and render it less sensitive to allergies. They are helpful in approximately 75% of the patients seen by a board certified veterinary dermatologist and allergy tested using an intradermal skin test. Most pet owners are able to learn how to give these injections.

FOOD ALLERGY

Food allergy is a relatively rare disease and generally overemphasized by many pet food companies as a cause of itching. The clinical signs may be sudden in onset and are virtually indistinguishable from those seen in allergic inhalant dermatitis. Sometimes, diarrhea is noted with food allergy. The symptoms are not usually associated with a change in diet, may start at any age and do not vary with the time of year or season. Many food-allergic dogs also have inhalant allergies and therefore may currently or previously exhibit some variability in severity of the disease depending on the season. Although food allergy is rare, it is an important allergy to consider because, unlike airborne allergies, it is possible to eliminate the

allergy causing substance(s) from the pet's environment. Control of the allergic disease is usually possible without the use of drugs.

Various tests are available for assistance in diagnosing food allergy. However, neither blood tests or the skin tests are very helpful in confirming the diagnosis. While positive reactions are often seen, they are usually not clinically important. False positive reactions may lead to the incorrect belief that a pet is very "food allergic." Negative reactions offer slightly more useful information and may indicate that a pet can likely tolerate a specific food substance. Most veterinary dermatologists do not recommend blood tests or skin tests for the diagnosis of food allergy. The best way to diagnose a food allergy is with the proper use of a hypoallergenic diet. Manufacturer claims that a diet contains certain substances does not indicate that the diet is truly hypoallergenic.

In order for an animal to be allergic to a food substance, the animal must have been exposed to the substance before. Lamb is a good example. There is absolutely nothing magical about lamb and food allergy. Simply, most dogs have not eaten lamb before and therefore cannot be allergic to it. A dog that has eaten lamb as part of its normal diet may actually be allergic to lamb. For years, lamb has been recommended by veterinarians as alternative to beef or chicken as a protein source in the diet of dogs suspected of having food allergy.

Unfortunately, the indiscriminate use of lamb in many dog foods, including puppy foods, has further complicated the necessary steps required to diagnose food allergy. Some dog foods advertised as "lamb and rice" also contain corn and poultry by-products, as well as other potential allergens commonly found in more "routine" types of diets. A well-

Identifying food allergies requires strict adherence to a food regimen in order to isolate the source of the irritant.

A properly balanced diet that includes plenty of fresh, clean water should be all that a dog needs to stay in fit condition.

meaning pet owner may try to perform a hypoallergenic dietary trial by changing from a "routine" diet to one of the "lamb and rice" diets that also contain food substances to which the pet may actually be allergic.

Careful reading of ingredients lists and a consultation with a veterinarian or veterinary dermatologist is often helpful in avoid this mistake.

Before initiating a hypoallergenic diet, a pet owner must understand that it is a true diagnostic test and should not be undertaken without conviction. Many times a hypoallergenic dietary trial is not strictly followed, and the pet is allowed to be exposed to table scraps or beef flavored treats, rawhides, and chew toys. Vitamin supplements and medications such as heartworm preventatives that contain meat flavorings should be substituted with a comparable product that does not contain these potential allergens. Failure to observe these requirements invalidates the test and results in unnecessarily exposing the pet to another potentially allergenic substance, such as lamb. This unnecessary exposure may preclude the use of such substances from utilization in the future when a more strictly followed hypoallergenic diet is considered.

In animals with concurrent allergies to pollens, it may be advisable to perform the hypoallergenic diet during a time of year when the symptoms are less likely due to those airborne allergens. The hypoallergenic diet should be continued until the dog improves, or for a duration of eight to ten weeks. If a pet improves while eating a hypoallergenic diet, the original diet should be reintroduced and the pet monitored for the return of itching within seven to fourteen days. Sometimes the itching may return within a matter of hours. This reintroduction of the original diet is a critical part of the test, and helps prove that the improvement was due to the food and not due to coincidence.

Once a food allergy is confirmed in this manner, the patient should be placed back on the successful hypoallergenic diet until the itching is no longer present. The dog may be maintained on this diet (provided it is well-balanced and complete) or placed on another diet and monitored for recurrence of itching. It is at this time that the use of diets, which have not undergone true clinical trials proving their hypoallergenic nature, may be considered for the individual pet. Introduction of potential allergenic substances may also be added individually to the proven hypoallergenic diet. This protocol allows for more precise identification of the offending food substance.

TREATMENT FOR THE ITCHY DOG

Various means of decreasing itch should be considered if the underlying reason for the sensation cannot be identified or while waiting for test results. It is important to remember that more than one disease may be contributing to itching. If identification and treatment for one of the causes does not result in adequate improvement, other causes should also be considered. Sometimes, the treatment of a specific disease may require some time until becoming effective. In these situations, or in cases involving an unidentified cause, nonspecific treatment for itching should be considered.

Both topical therapy (shampoos, sprays, lotions and creams) and systemic therapy (medications given by mouth) can be useful. The use of drugs other than steroids to control itching is less convenient, but reduces the potential for serious side effects, especially when long term therapy is needed. If these other drugs are not totally effective in controlling clinical signs, they often help reduce the amount of steroids that are necessary to decrease itching.

Some patients require a combination of immunotherapy injections, antihistamines, fatty acids, and even intermittent steroids in order to maintain an adequate comfort level without incurring side effects due to overuse of one drug. The costs of antihistamines and fatty acids are usually greater than the costs of steroids. However, the costs of side effects and diseases associated with excessive steroid use, can be substantial in both monetary and health-related terms. For medium to large sized dogs with allergic inhalant dermatitis, the cost of immunotherapy injections administered by the pet owner is often less that the cost of most forms of medical control. The importance of identifying the underlying cause for itching cannot be overemphasized.

Spending time with you dog is beneficial for you both, and it can also give you the opportunity to check your pet's coat for any signs of trouble.

OTHER COMMON PROBLEMS

Many different types of diseases can affect the skin directly and indirectly. There are various ways to classify skin problems or symptoms. Classically, diseases are grouped by their cause. However, it may be equally important to consider other factors. For the patient's and pet owner's sake, it is often appropriate to group the diseases based on the likelihood of a particular disease being present. Additionally, the cost and invasiveness of the tests that may be necessary to confirm a diagnosis are often a consideration. The length of time that may be required to confirm the diagnosis and/or achieve a cure is also a factor. The presence of concurrent disease or complicating factors may affect the recommended treatments and the order in which diagnostic tests are performed. Some symptoms may be the result of a disease that causes skin problems as well as problems in other parts of the body (such as internal organs). It may be helpful to group diseases according to their history and which symptoms occurred first (itching, a rash, or hair loss). Often, the symptoms have been present for so long or are so varied that it may be difficult to remember the progression of disease.

Various skin problems look very much alike. Fortunately, the more common infections or mite infestations either respond relatively quickly to

Since many bacterial infections look alike, it is important to run the required diagnostic tests. Bacterial infections can sometimes be mistaken for hives, and although certain circular areas of hair loss look remarkably like ringworm, they may in fact be something else entirely.

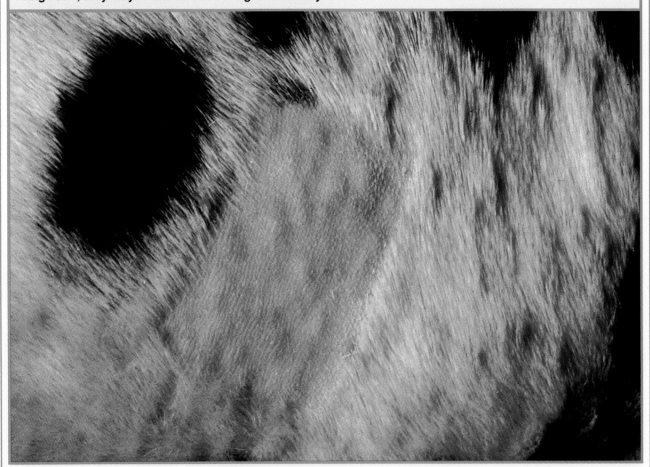

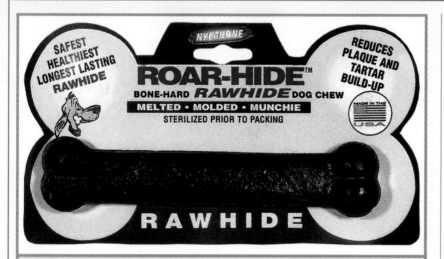

To combat boredom and relieve your dog's natural desire to chew, there's nothing better than a Roar-Hide. Unlike common rawhide, this bone won't turn into a gooey mess when chewed, so your dog won't choke on small pieces of it, and your carpet won't be stained by it. The Roar-Hide is completely edible and is high in protein.

treatment and do not require particularly invasive or expensive tests to confirm the diagnosis. These diseases may be present by themselves or in association with other more complex and difficult to treat (and diagnose) diseases. It may be necessary to treat the more common and apparant disease before pursuing further diagnostic tests or treatments. In some situations, it is necessary to treat for several suspected and confirmed disease at the same time in a single patient. The possibility that the general health of the body may be affected suggests that tests be performed to make sure that diseases (such as diabetes, liver or kidney abnormalities or problems with red blood cells or white blood cells) are not present.

INFECTIONS

Infections are often associated with odor, but may or may not cause itching. Bacterial infections are especially common and are often related to an underlying problem such as an allergy or hormonal imbalance. The most common bacterial agent identified in superficial skin infections is *Staphylococcus intermedius*. The most well-known fungal infection is called "ringworm." The use of the word "worm" is confusing because worms have nothing to do with this disease. Yeast infections affecting the skin are increasingly being identified. Fortunately, it is a relatively straightforward process to diagnose and treat most bacterial and yeast infections. The challenging cases are those that have a coexisting complicating disease, extend deeper into the skin and subcutaneous tissue, or seem to be recurrent. The emotions and frustrations that pet owners feel in these situations is similar to what parents must feel when their child suffers from chronic or recurrent ear infections.

Although itching is not always present, hair loss can be seen with any of these infections. Most pets with circular areas of hair loss actually have a bacterial infection rather than ringworm. Rashes or a bad odor are also seen with bacteria as well as yeast. Ringworm seldom causes an odor, but is often associated with hair loss and, less commonly, a rash. If a dog suffers recurrent infections of any type, the possibility of an underlying cause should be considered. The chronic use of steroids and the inflamed skin associated with allergies or other diseases also predisposes a dog to infections.

Most of these organisms are not contagious, but are commonly found in the environment, often even in small numbers on your pet. However, ringworm can be transmitted among pets and people. Some animals, especially cats, can be nonsymptomatic (not show any symptoms) carriers of the ringworm-causing organism. This means that they do not show any symptoms of an infection, but are capable of passing it along to other animals or people. Children, the elderly, and people with comprised immunities are more susceptible to this disease, but anyone can catch it. The organism may even be transmitted by inanimate objects, such as bedding materials, towels or brushes.

The diagnosis of the various types of infections can often be made based upon the history of the dog and by physical examination. The use of a microscope to examine samples obtained from the skin may be necessary to confirm the suspected diagnosis, and ensure that other infections are not present. Occasionally, cultures or skin biopsies may be necessary. In some situations, your veterinarian may refer you and your pet to a board certified veterinary dermatologist for another opinion and treatment recommendations.

In complex skin diseases, your veterinarian or veterinary dermatologist may recommend reevaluating your pet during or after the use of drug therapy, to ensure that the original problem has been brought under control, and to see what the remaining condition looks like without secondary infections. In order to make sure that an infection has cleared entirely, repeat examinations and tests may be necessary. Sometimes the symptoms may appear to have totally improved but the disease is still present to a much lesser extent. In such cases longer term therapy may be needed. It can be difficult to determine if the problem is still present or if something else is contributing to the symptoms.

Sharing a home with a pet suffering from a recurring skin problem can be psychologically and financially challenging, especially when multiple problems are present. For you and your pet's sake, it is important to share your concerns with your veterinarian and understand that your pet may have a disease that is incurable, but, with time and the proper treatment, can be controlled and managed.

HAIR LOSS AND HORMONAL DISEASES

Hair loss can occur with both hormonal and non-hormonal diseases. If your pet is not causing the hair loss by chewing, itching, licking, or rubbing, and does not have an infection, then a hormonal disease may be the reason. Other causes include an unbalanced diet, stress, genetic diseases and in rare cases, skin cancer.

Most hormonal diseases are not typically associated with significant itching unless they have predisposed a patient to an infection which, in turn, has caused itching. However, sometimes the combination of dry skin and a dry environment can lead a pet with a hormonal disease to exhibit itching. There is also a syndrome, called *calcinosis cutis*, associated with the hormonal disease, Cushing's disease, which can be quite itchy. Hypothyroidism is the most well known hormonal disease, but not every dog with hair loss is hypothyroid.

Your veterinarian or veterinary dermatologist may rely on a combination of clinical signs, history, special blood tests, skin biopsies and other tests to determine which disease(s) may be present.

HYPOTHYROIDISM

Hypothyroidism refers to the lack of thyroid hormone present in the body and its interaction with the individual cells of the body. "Hypo" means less or too little. Thyroid hormone is important in the general health of a pet, as well as to the skin and immune system. The production of this hormone is controlled by a small gland near

Dogs will sometimes lick or itch themselves out of boredom—but not if they have safe, durable chew toys like this to distract them.

the brain that sends signals the thyroid gland found in the neck. The thyroid gland produces thyroid hormone that is then distributed throughout the body via the blood stream. In most cases, the cause of hypothyroidism cannot be determined. However, some forms of the disease may have a genetic basis.

The clinical signs of hypothyroidism are quite variable and the more obvious symptoms are seldom noted initially. Recurrent skin infections and a poor hair coat are the more common signs. The hair coat may be sparse, dull, dry, and scaly, or may become oily. Itching is usually not a prominent symptom unless another disease is also present such as allergies or some infections. Pets may not want to play and exercise or have as much energy as they once did. Weight gain may be seen in some pets, but is not particularly common.

The diagnosis of hypothyroidism is not always apparent. Blood tests are useful but not always definitive. It may be necessary to test for blood levels of various substances associated with the functioning of the thyroid gland or repeat the test again at a later date. The treatment for hypothyroidism is usually relatively straightforward. Initial improvement should be noted in two to four weeks, but it may be months before all the changes associated with this disease are no longer noticeable. Thyroid replacement therapy and reevaluation of the blood levels will be necessary for the rest of the pet's life.

STEROID-RELATED DISEASE

As discussed in the medication section of this book, there are different types of steroids. The diseases associated with steroids can be due to either excessive or a lack of steroids. An excess of corticosteroids (called Cushing's disease or hyperadrenocorticism) is the most common steroid-associated disease.

The disease may be caused by an abnormality within the body itself and, if so, is called endogenous. If the disease is the result of the administration of steroids by injections, by mouth (or even in very rare cases by application to the

This dog was diagnosed with both Cushing's disease and hypothyroidism. Due to proper diagnosis and treatment by a veterinary dermatologist, further improvement was noted with continual therapy, and an increase in activity and mental alertness was also apparent.

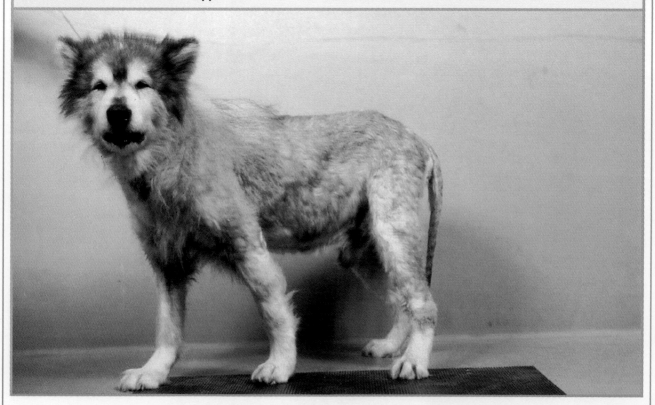

Your dog can fully enjoy the wonders of nature if you simply implement a few preventative measures.

When you go to the trouble and time to maximize your dog's health by feeding a diet with the highest quality ingredients, don't skimp on biscuits or you could have a problem anyway. Photo courtesy of Nature's Recipe Pet Foods.

skin or ears) it is referred to as being iatrogenic, meaning "the result of certain treatment." Prudent and limited use of corticosteroids rarely causes problems and, as discussed in the chapter, on medication, can be very useful in treating many skin diseases. Unfortunately, it is not uncommon for some diseases to lead to an overuse of this group of drugs.

Endogenous hyperadrenocorticism may be caused by a problem within the glands of the body that produce the steroids. The glands are called the adrenal glands and are located near each kidney. The disease may also be due to a problem with the part of the brain that controls the adrenal glands.

Various blood tests, urine tests, x-rays, and ultrasound examinations may be necessary to find out if the disease is present. The preliminary tests are usually screening tests that are used to determine if the disease is present. Additional tests may be performed to differentiate which type of

hyperadrenocorticism is present. These additional tests may be necessary to help decide which type of treatment is preferable.

The symptoms of excess steroids in the body are virtually the same as the side effects of steroids that are discussed in the medications chapter. Sometimes they may come on so slowly that they are confused with the normal aging process. Some pet owners report that it is almost like having a puppy again and that they did not realize how "unhealthy" or "tired" or "old" their pet had been acting.

The treatment of iatrogenic Cushing's disease involves slowly decreasing and tapering the use of steroid being administered to the pet. In most cases, it is important to slowly decrease the dose of steroids in order to give the body a chance to adjust and start producing its own appropriate levels of this necessary hormone. The levels produced by the body are much less that the levels usually seen when steroids are being used to treat a

disease. Decreasing steroid use may require that the underlying reason for the original use of steroid be further investigated. If this is not possible or practical, the use of other drugs to control the original symptoms may be necessary. The treatment of endogenous Cushing's disease is quite complicated and there are several options that your veterinarian, veterinary dermatologist or veterinary internist may discuss with you. Cushing's disease itself can be life-threatening, but so can the treatment as well. Fortunately, most patients do well, but frequent reevaluations are often necessary.

The opposite of having too high a level of steroids in the body is having too little. Most cases involve mineralocorticoids rather that glucocorticoids. It is considered to be a rare disease, but probably affects more dogs than we realize. This disease can be life-threatening and quite varied in symptoms. However, it is important not to use this

This dog has a severe case of ringworm which affects a large part of the body, although it was especially severe on the leg area.

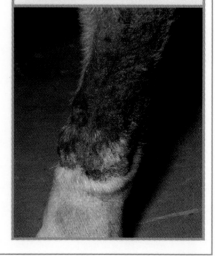

SND (Superficial Necrolytic Dermatitis) of the feet. This pet suffers from a rare liver disease that results in a severe skin trauma associated with sec–ondary bacterial and yeast infections.

diagnosis as a "scapegoat" for a pet suffering from a variety of vague symptoms. Skin-related symptoms are actually seldom noted. Just because a patient improves with prednisone therapy does not mean that the patient has a disease due to a lack of steroids being produced by the body.

IMMUNE MEDIATED OR AU-TOIMMUNE DISEASES

This group of diseases is among the most heartbreaking due to the often severe symp-toms affecting the skin and, in some cases, other parts of the body. Perhaps the most well-known disease is "lupus" that is also seen in people. Symp-toms are not always noted in the skin, but are sometimes apparant. Pemphigus is actu-ally the most common im-mune-mediated disease affect-ing the skin of dogs and usually only affects the skin. However, the affected animal may act systematically ill.

Skin-related symptoms may include sores and scabs. The feet, mouth, nose, and the areas around the eyes and genitals are often the first to be affected. In severe cases, it may appear that part of the skin or foot pads have sloughed off. Patients may or may not become systematically ill.

The actual cause of this group of diseases is not known. Genetics, drugs, hormones, sun exposure, and other factors seem to play a role in some cases. The basic biology involves the actions of the body's immune system against the skin or other body organs, such as the kidneys or blood.

Diagnosis may involve several tests. It is important to make sure that other more common diseases are not present. These other diseases may look similar to an im-mune-mediated disease or be present at the same time. They can complicate the diagnosis and treatment. Bloodwork and relatively non-invasive procedures may be the first tests performed before a skin biopsy is pur-sued. The blood test may also be necessary before initiating some forms of treatment because of the potential side effects of treatment. When a biopsy is performed, we are only getting a picture of what is happening at that moment in that small section of skin.

Site selection is very impor-tant when determining which specific location to biopsy. The biopsy may best be read by a veterinary dermatologist with a special interest in skin biopsies or veterinary patholo-gist with a special interest in dermatological diseases. Even with meticulous care, an absolute diagnosis is not always possible, and repeat biopsies may be necessary.

If the diagnosis of an im-mune-mediated disease is made, then high-dose steroids, or other drugs that suppress the immune system, may be used to control the symptoms. Because of the life-threatening nature of immune-mediated diseases, and the potential side effects associated with their treatment, follow up tests and regular reevaluations by your veterinarian or veterinary dermatologist are often neces-sary.

SEBORRHEA

This "disease" is really a symptom in most cases and may be due to a variety of causes. When seborrhea is caused by another disease, the term "secondary seborrhea" is used. Most of these causes are discussed above and elsewhere in this book. If an underlying cause cannot be determined, the term "primary seborrhea" or "idiopathic seborrhea" is used.

If your pet has seborrhea, it is important to try to find an underlying reason, because

The same dog, showing SND on the face.

treatment for idiopathic seborrhea can be quite unrewarding. Allergies, hormonal imbalances, parasites, infections, skin cancer, and other diseases should be considered. The term "primary seborrhea" is used if tests for do not indicate an underlying cause for the symptoms and a skin biopsy is compatible with the diagnosis of primary seborrhea. Your veterinarian or veterinary dermatologist will likely try to make sure that that no other disease is present and complicating the symptoms before selecting a location to biopsy.

The clinical signs of seborrhea vary greatly among individuals. Symptoms ranging from dry flakes to excessive oiliness or greasiness are common. The situation can be quite confusing because infections can make a pet look and smell as if primary seborrhea is present, and patients with primary seborrhea are prone to secondary infections. A bad odor may be the result of a skin infection or seborrhea itself.

If an underlying reason for the symptoms cannot be determined, lifelong therapy will likely be necessary.

Treatment options usually center around controlling the secondary infections and shampoo therapy. In some cases, other medications ranging from naturally occurring and synthetic vitamin A-type drugs, to even steroids, may be helpful. Primary seborrhea is almost never associated with life-threatening complications. However, the "high maintenance" nature and varied success methods used in controlling the symptoms, can lead to a poor quality of life for all members of the household.

It is important to read the labels of all shampoo-related products before using them on your dog. A shampoo that is appropriate for a cat may not work for your dog, so make certain of the suitability for your own pet before you buy.

MEDICATIONS AND SUPPLEMENTS

Medications are an important part of helping to treat a pet's skin problems. Both topical therapy (shampoos, sprays, lotions and creams) and systemic therapy (medications given by mouth or injections) are often utilized. Some topical medications are strong enough to have systemic actions and side effects. The following section will discuss sytemic medications such as steroids, antihistamines, fatty acids, antibiotics, and thyroid replacment therapy.

STEROIDS

Perhaps the most useful and potentialy abused systemic medication used to treat certain skin disorders is the group of drugs known as steroids. The types of steroids used to treat skin problems in animals is different than the types of steroids most people think of in association with human body builders. Anabolic steroids are used by humans to increase lean muscle mass, and are associated with many potential side effects. Glucocorticoids (corticosteroids) are in a different class of steroids and are used in animals as well as humans to control inflamation, itching and to supress the immune system. They have many actions and are useful in a variety of diseases. Unfortunately, they also have numerous potential side effects.

Steroids are the most well-known drug used to control itching and are an important part of the treatment of immune-mediated diseases, such as pemphigus and lupus. They also may go by names such as cortisone, prednisone, methylprednisone, triamcinolone, and may be administered in pill form or by injection. This group of drugs is effective in controlling many of the causes of itching in dogs but have significant long-term and not always obvious side effects. Short-term side effects include aggressive behavior, increased water consumption, increased urination ("accidents" in the house), increased appetite, panting, pancreatitis (which may be life-threatening), and sometimes stomach ulcers. Long-term side effects are many and varied. Basically, the steroids act to inhibit the body from producing its own steroids. This upsets the normal hormonal balance. Other side effects include weight gain, behavior changes, liver damage, poor hair coat, demodectic mange, thin skin, comedones (blackheads) and hair loss. The body's defenses are compromised and bladder or skin infections are common.

The side effects can occur slowly over time and may make the dog appear as if premature aging is occurring. Some patient's diseases may appear to become resistant to steroids after long-term use. This is because of a secondary infection or the occurrance of another disease. Once the infection or other disease has been controlled, the itch may once again be responsive to the same steroid. However, it may be necessary to change the type of steroid being used to treat a particular disease. Obviously if these problems have been noted, the use of steroids should be reduced or eliminated.

To help decrease potential side effects with long term use, daily administration of steroids should be avoided. However, some diseases are so severe that daily use of steroids is necessary. In most cases, prednisone should not be given more frequently than once every 48 hours for long-term use. Triamcinolone remains in the body slightly longer than prednisone and should not be given more frequently than every three days if chronic use is required.

Even when these guidelines are followed, many animals will still have side effects, although usually to a lesser degree. For this reason, long-term steroid injections to help reduce itching for several weeks should be avoided. Symptoms may actually return before the injectable steroid has entirely worked its way out of the dogs system.

Long-term side effects are more likely with injections than pills. However, chronic use of steroid pills can also lead to serious side effects. Another advantage of the pill formulation is that if your pet gets sick and should not be given any more steroids, most pill formulations will be out of the dog's system after a day or

Check with your veterinarian before introducing a new food—even a healthy one—to your pet's diet.

two. Once a long-term injection of a steroid is administered, the drug remains in the body for a longer amount of time, and and cannot be removed.

Steroids provide a very important form of therapy. If used wisely, they are usually safe. Short-term use seldom causes serious problems. If steroids are needed for months or years, other options should be considered. As always, it is best to have a diagnosis and identify an underlying reason for the symptoms before using steroids. This is especially important when long-term use of these drugs is necessary. For this reason, many pet owners may be referred to a board certified veterinary dermatologist.

Severe, life threatening diseases may require very high doses of steroids and your veterinarian or veterinary dermatologist may consider using other drugs to suppress the immune system. These other drugs include azathioprine, chlorambucil,

gold therapy or a variety of other drugs. These drugs are associated with various side effects that can lead to a sudden life-threating situation. They may be used in conjunction with steroids to help lower the dose of each type of drug necessary to control the symptoms. Recently, the combined use of certain antibiotics (tetracycline, erythromycin) and the nutritional supplement, niacinamide, (not to be confused with niacin, which is different) has been found to be useful in some types of diseases.

ANTIHISTAMINES AND FATTY ACIDS

In addition to steroids, there are other drugs that can be utilized to help decrease the inflamation associated with itching and itching itself. These options include antihistamines and fatty acids. In order to understand how medical therapy is effective, it helps to think of three separate and individual pathways that lead to inflammation and itching. Steroids block all three path-

ways, but because of their side effects, drugs that block the individual pathway should be considered.

Antihistamines include drugs such as hydroxyzine, diphenhydramine, chlorpheniramine, Seldane® and Tavist®. They help block only one of the three main pathways that lead to inflammation and itching. Antihistamines work better as a preventative measure, but they can be used on an as-needed basis if the itching has not become severe. Although generally safe, this group of drugs can have side effects such as sedation, excitation and an increased risk of siezures in pets who are predisposed to this condition. They should *not* be used without consulting a veterinarian.

Drugs with psychological actions can also be helpful in controling itch. Doxepin and Amitriptyline, a drug used as an antidepressant in humans, have rather potent antihistaminic actions in dogs, and can be as beneficial as antihistamines in treating allergy-induced itching in many pets. Prozac® has been used successfully in treating some dogs with a syndrome know as "lick granuloma" or acral lick dermatitis. It has received a disproportionate degree of publicity as to its usefulness in treating skin problems. Diazepam (Valium®) has also been beneficial in some cases.

Fatty acids are available in powder, liquid and capsule formulations. They help block another of the individual pathways that lead to inflammation, but may require six to eight weeks of use until maximum effectiveness is observed. Fatty acids work better as an preventative method, rather than to stop the inflammation once it has become a problem. They also help control dry or flaky skin which can also cause itching. There are many different brand names of this type of drug. The optimum ratio of specific ingredients has yet to be determined. Label claims of greater quantities of essential ingredients do not necessarily correlate with a greater success rate. The use of formulations which have undergone clinical trials proving their efficacy is recommended.

The use of drugs other than steroids to control itching is less convenient, but reduces the potential for serious side effects. If these other drugs are not totally effective in controlling clinical signs, they often can help reduce the amount of steroids that are necessary to decrease itching. The costs of antihistamines and fatty acids are usually greater than the costs of steroids. However the costs of side effects and diseases associated with excessive steroid use can be substantial in both monetary and health-related terms. For patients with allergic inhalant dermatitis, the use of immunotherapy injections based on intradermal skin testing, may provide a cost-effective alternative. Some patients require a combination of various treatments in order to maintain an adequate comfort level without incurring side effects due to overuse of one drug. The importance of identifying the underlying and coexisting cause(s) for itching cannot be over emphasized. It is also important to note that the

original cause of the symptom may be different that the cause of the reappearance of the symptom. For instance, itching may originally be due to allergies. A reappearance of itching may be due to fleas or mites.

ANTIBIOTICS AND ANTIMICRO-BIAL DRUGS

Bacterial and yeast infections are common problems associated with many different types of skin diseases. While they may not be the pet's primary problem, identifing and treating for these infections is a very important component of improving the patient's condition. It is important to make sure that these medications are given as directed, and for the full amount of time prescribed. In complex skin diseases, your veterinarian or veterinary dermatologist may recommend reevaluating your pet after the use of these drugs to ensure that the infections have been brought under control, and to see what the remaing condition looks like without secondary infections complicating the overall symptoms.

There are many different types of antibiotics. When utilized to treat bacterial skin infections, they are usually used for a minimum duration of three weeks. Perhaps the most common side effect is an upset stomach or diarrhea and this can be seen with various types of antibiotics. Other adverse reactions are also possible, but fortunately life-threatening side effects are very uncommon. Bacteria may become resistant to a certain type of antibiotic that may require a substitute.

With long-term or repeated use, they may predispose a patient to a yeast infection. This is one example of why a reevaluation may be necessary. The recurrence of symptoms may be due to either a yeast infection or a return of the bacterial infection.

Yeast infections may occur in the ear as well as on the skin. There is often an underlying disease present and the infections can be a recurring problem. Some yeast infections can be controlled with topical therapy, while others require systemic medications. Topical medications range from a vinegar and water mixture to prescrition preparations. Prescription medications adminstered by mouth (such as ketoconazole) can be quite helpful, but are often expensive and can be associated with side effects, including liver problems. For these reasons, ketoconazole is seldom prescribed or refilled without confirmation of the diagnosis of yeast through the use a microscopic examination.

THYROID HORMONES

The primary use of thyroid replacment therapy is for pets who have been diagnosed with hypothroidism. Thyroid pills contain a hormone that replaces what the body is not producing. Animals metabolize and process this hormone differently than humans, so the dosage in dogs is usually quite different than the dosage appropriate for people of the same weight. Studies indicate that a twice-daily regimen is best, but some animals will be able to be maintained on a once a day dose.

All healthy dogs require the right balance of vitamins and minerals to ensure health from the inside-out.

Supplementation will likely be necessary for the rest of the patient's life. The initial dose is primarily based on the size of the patient, but may need to be altered because of individual variations and the stage of the disease. A "post pill thyroid test" should be perfomed approximately six weeks after starting thyroid replacment therapy. This involves taking a blood sample approximately four to six hours after administration of the pill. Side effects of this medication are quite rare, but some animals may become excitable, have trouble sleeping or go to the bathroom more frequently. If these side effects are noted, you should check with your veterinarian about changing the dose. A post-pill thyroid test is useful to help confirm the suspicion.

Once the correct dose is achieved, follow-up is recommend approximately every six to twelve months, or sooner if problems are noted.

VITAMINS AND MINERALS

Dogs fed a well-balanced and complete diet seldom benefit from additional vitamin supplements. Indescriminant supplementation can have potentially harmful effects, especially with the non-water soluble vitamins. However, many veterinarians and veterinary dermatologists recommend moderate doses of vitamin E as an aid in the treatment of a variety of diseases ranging from demodectic mange to discoid lupus. Naturally ocurring vitamin A is used to treat a very limited number of seborrhea patients, but

toxicity problems can occur.

The synthetic formulations of vitamin A are available only by prescription, and are more expensive, but are associated with fewer side effects. There are also a very limited number of zinc-related skin diseases that respond well to zinc supplementation. One should be careful when supplementing with vitamins and minerals as some of them have the potential to bind up, or compete with other vitamins and minerals, and may actually do more harm than good.

YEAST, GARLIC, SEAWEED, SHARK CARTILAGE AND OTHER SUPPLEMENTS

It seems that everytime you turn around, someone is recommending a new or all-natural supplement. Their recommendations are usually based on personal experience. While testimonials are important, good scientific studies are necessary to prove that the beneficial effects are due to the product rather than sheer coincidence or other factors.

Some of these products are based on scientific medicine, but that does not mean that the product as a whole is good. Fortunately, most of these supplements have minimal side effects. It is perfectly understandable to want to try some of these therapies because of the chronic and often incurable nature of many skin problems. Without scientific studies, it is difficult to determine which products I would recommend. Admittedly, my medical training has been in the traditional sciences, but I do believe that there is a great

deal that has yet to be discovered, and I feel certain that new medications and treatments will continue to be discovered to improve the quality of life for our animal friends. The most effective therapies of the future will be based on good science, and will be able to withstand the scrutiniy of numerous researchers as well as patients.

SUMMARY

The preceding discussion of various medications and supplements is by no means complete or a substitute for veterinary care. With virtually all drugs, side effects are possible, and these should be discussed with your veterinarian. Life-threatening reactions are rare, but can potentially occur with any drug. Even drugs that are available over-the-counter can have devas-

tating side effects. In some cases, the symptoms of a particular disease and the signs of side effects of a certain medication may be very similar. A reevaluation by a veterinarian or veterinary dermatologist may reveal the presence of a new disease, a drug related side effects or the recurrence of a previously controlled disease. Often follow-up examinations and tests are necessary to make sure that the original problem has cleared. Sometimes the symptoms may appear to have improved completely but the disease is still present to a much reduced degree. Longer term therapy may be needed. Without follow-up, it can be difficult to determine if the original problem is still present or if something else is contributing to the symptoms.

Placing your dog's dish down for twenty minutes each mealtime will keep him in a regular routine.

SUGGESTED READING

TS-249
SKIN AND COAT CARE
FOR YOUR DOG

TS-214
OWNER'S GUIDE TO DOG HEALTH

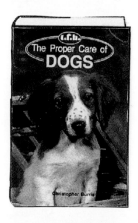

TW-102
THE PROPER CARE OF DOGS

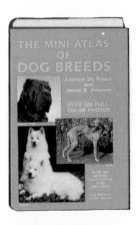

H-1106
THE MINI-ATLAS OF DOGS

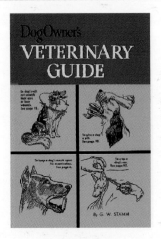

AP-927
DOG OWNER'S VETERINARY GUIDE

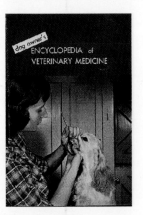

H-934
DOG OWNER'S ENCYCLOPEDIA OF
VETERINARY MEDICINE

Acknowledgement

This volume in the Basic Training, Caring & Understanding Library series was researched in part at the Ontario Veterinary college at the University of Guelph in Guelph, Ontario, and was published under the auspices of Dr. Herbert R. Axelrod.

A world-renown scientist, explorer, author, university professor, lecturer, and publisher, Dr. Axelrod is the best-known tropical fish expert in the world and the founder and chairman of T.F.H. Publications, Inc., the largest and most respected publisher of pet literature in the world. He has written 16 definitive texts on Ichthyology (including the best-selling Handbook of Tropical Aquarium Fishes), published more than 30 books on individual species of fish for the hobbyist, written hundreds of articles, and discovered hundreds of previously unknown species, six of which have been named after him.

Dr. Axelrod holds a Ph.D and was awarded an Honorary Doctor of Science degree by the University of Guelph, where he is now an adjunct professor in the Department of Zoology. He has served on the American Pet Products Manufacturers Association Board of Governors and is a member of the American Society of Herpetologists and Ichthyologists, the Biometric Society, the New York Zoological Society, the New York Academy of Sciences, the American Fisheries Society, the National Research Council, the National Academy of Sciences, and numerous aquarium societies around the world. In 1977, Dr. Axelrod was awarded the Smithson Silver Medal for his ichthyological and charitable endeavors by the Smithsonian Institution. A decade later, he was elected an endowment member of the American Museum of Natural History and was named a life member of the James Smithson Society by the Smithsonian Associates' national board. He has donated in excess of $50 million in recent years to the American Museum of National History, the University of Guelph, and other institutions.

Index